Listen to the Pause

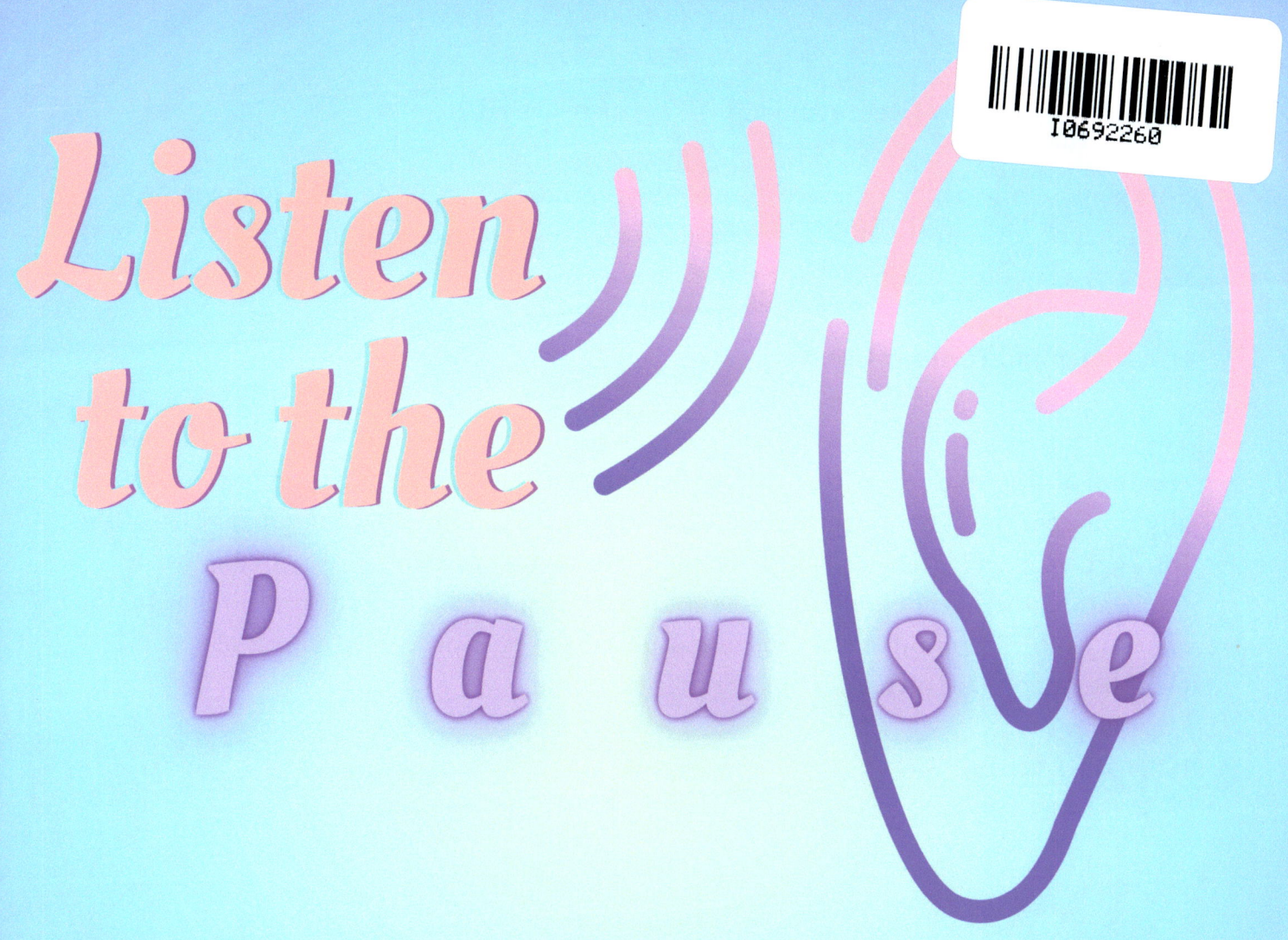

Part of *Tara's Life Unscripted* series

Tara Ijai & Deedra Abboud

Disclaimer and Terms of Use:

The Author and Publisher has strived to be as accurate and complete as possible in the creation of this book, notwithstanding the fact that she does not warrant or represent at any time that the contents within are accurate due to the rapidly changing nature of the Internet. While all attempts have been made to verify information provided in this publication, the Author and Publisher assume no responsibility for errors, omissions, or contrary interpretation of the subject matter herein. Any perceived slights of specific persons, peoples, or organizations are unintentional.

ISBN 978-1-956565-40-9

This book is dedicated to:

Love Rebels
on a journey of
personal discovery and growth.

May embracing your true self bring you joy!

In the bustling city of Baytown, where the sun danced on skyscraper windows and the streets buzzed with life, Tara found herself navigating a maze of appointments and responsibilities.

Yet amidst the chaos, she stumbled upon a pivotal moment that would change her outlook forever.

It began with a simple request —
two different medical images,
two different appointments.

Tara knew it would be
a logistical challenge,
but she dared to voice her needs,
hoping for a stroke of luck.

As fate would have it,
her insurance coordinator
was her ally,
orchestrating a three-way call
with the lab and
their scheduler, Carlos.

Carlos, diligent yet
constrained by time,
proposed a solution:
both images scheduled together,
albeit a several weeks later.

Tara hesitated,
her mind weighing the options.

A voice inside her
whispered acceptance,
rationalizing the wait against the
backdrop of enduring pain.

And she agreed to the dates
far in the future.

**But then,
a beacon of empathy
shone through the phone line –
her coordinator's gentle inquiry
pierced the silence.**

"Tara, I heard you pause," her coordinator's voice rang with concern.

"Is this date really okay for you, given your struggle with pain?"

It was a moment of revelation, a pivotal juncture where Tara realized the importance of advocating for herself.

She smiled, feeling the warmth
of her coordinator's support like a
guardian angel at her side.

With newfound resolve,
she spoke up,
requesting separate appointments
for swifter access to answers.

Carlos, ever obliging,
swiftly rearranged the schedule,
with appointments on different days
but both sooner,
leaving Tara in awe
of the power of her own voice.

Gratitude swelled within her as she thanked her coordinator for her keen observation and unwavering support.

I matter

In that exchange,
Tara gleaned a profound lesson –
the act of asking for what one needs
is a profound form of self-love.

As the call concluded,
Tara found herself reflecting on the
significance of the encounter.

Her coordinator's words
echoed in her mind,
a gentle reminder that
being nice and being pliable
are not synonymous.

NICE

≠

PLIABLE

It was a lesson in self-advocacy, in honoring one's needs unapologetically.

In the days that followed,
Tara carried that lesson with her,
a beacon of empowerment
guiding her through
life's twists and turns.

She learned to listen
not only to her own pauses
but to those of others,
recognizing the universal struggle
to prioritize self-care in a world
that often demands self-sacrifice.

And so, in the bustling
city of Baytown,
amidst the cacophony of daily life,
Tara discovered a
quiet strength within herself –
the power to speak up,
to ask for what she needed,
and to love herself enough
to prioritize her own well-being.

For in the end, she realized,
every act of self-advocacy
is a testament to the resilience
of the human spirit and
the boundless capacity
for growth and healing.

Find your own
wearable affirmations at
MyLoveGlasses.com:

@LoveGlassesRevolution

www.ingramcontent.com/pod-product-compliance
Lightning Source LLC
Chambersburg PA
CBHW041003170626
46815CB00002B/133